Garfield
to the
Rescue

Written by Jim Kraft
Illustrated by Brett Koth
and Larry Fentz, Paws, Inc.

ISBN 0-89954-565-3

 Antioch Publishing Company
Yellow Springs, Ohio 45387

One afternoon Garfield was playing "Squash the Dog" outside with Odie when a van stopped and a strange man jumped out.

"What a nice doggy and kitty," said the man, patting the pets on the head. "Would you like to go to the park with me?"

Garfield backed away. "We don't go with strangers."

"I'll give you these," the man continued, holding out a handful of pet treats.

"I'm not hungry," replied Garfield. "Gee, I can't believe I said that!"

Odie stepped up to sniff the treats.

Suddenly the man grabbed Odie. "Drop that dog!" cried Garfield, clutching Odie's tail. But the man yanked Odie away, causing Garfield to tumble backwards. Then the stranger tossed Odie into the van and drove away!

"Dognapper! Dognapper! Help!" shouted Garfield. He chased the van as far as he could. But, Garfield being a fat cat, that wasn't very far.

Garfield collapsed on the sidewalk. As he was catching his breath, Zeke, a neighbor's cat, walked by. Garfield told Zeke what had happened.

"That's bad," said Zeke. "Sounds like the work of the Petman."

"The Petman? Who's that?" asked Garfield.

"The most notorious petnapper of them all," explained Zeke, with a shudder. "He steals all kinds of pets, and their owners never see them again. They say he has a hideout near the docks. Smart cats stay away from there."

"Thanks for the advice," said Garfield grimly. "But this smart cat has to rescue a dopey dog."

The dockyard district was a jumble of dark alleys and grimy warehouses. It was such a tough neighborhood, even the rats were afraid to go out at night.

One old warehouse seemed deserted, its windows boarded up. But inside were rows of cages filled with sad, frightened pets.

The Petman's van rolled into the warehouse and was greeted by an evil-looking Doberman. The Petman dragged Odie from the van.

"Look at this mutt, Pitch," the Petman said. "He's got a face only a flea could love. I'll be lucky to get two dollars for him." He shoved Odie into a cage. "If I can't sell him, maybe you'd like to eat him, eh?" The Petman laughed loudly.

Pitch grinned at Odie and licked his lips.

Odie rested his chin on his paws and whimpered softly.

"Polly wants a cracker!" someone squawked.

Odie looked up. A parrot in the next cage was speaking to him.

"Sorry, I don't know why I said that," the parrot explained. "But I can't seem to help myself. I hear things and I repeat them. To be honest, I don't even like crackers. And my name's not Polly. It's Tia. But everyone calls me Polly. I can't figure it out."

Odie stopped sniffling and smiled weakly.

"So, how do you like being petnapped?" asked the parrot.

Odie gave a long, mournful howl.

"I know just what you mean," said Tia.

Meanwhile, Garfield was crisscrossing the dockyard area in search of Odie. He approached a rat lounging on a street corner.

"I'm looking for the Petman," said Garfield. "Know where I can find him?"

"Maybe. Maybe not," said the rat. "What's it worth to you?"

"I don't have any money," replied Garfield.

"Well, what do you have?"

"I have an idea," said Garfield. "You tell me what you know, and I don't use you for a chew toy."

The rat gulped. "That sounds fair."

According to the rat, the Petman's hideout was in an old lasagna factory somewhere close by. Using his pasta-sensitive nose, Garfield was able to locate the building in no time.

Garfield pried one of the boards away from a window and squeezed through. He crept through the factory until he saw the rows of cages.

"Odie, old pal! I've found you!" cried Garfield, rushing up to Odie's cage and hugging him through the bars.

"Polly wants a cracker!" squawked Tia.

"We're having a special moment here, if you don't mind," said Garfield.

"Oh, I said it again, didn't I," replied Tia. "So sorry. Listen, you'd better get out of here before the Petman returns."

"I'm not leaving without Odie," replied Garfield. "Where's the key to these cages?"

"In there," said Tia, pointing to a door. "On a hook beside the Petman's bed. There's just one problem."

"What's that?" asked Garfield.

Suddenly Garfield heard a low, sinister growl.

"Never mind," said Garfield. "I think I can guess."

Garfield turned and found himself facing Pitch's menacing fangs.

"Uh, gee, what great teeth," said Garfield. "You must floss regularly, huh? Well, I'd love to stay, but you probably have to eat a car or something, so I'll just run along."

And run Garfield did! Pitch chased him over crates and conveyor belts, under pipes and pulleys, and all around the factory. The fat cat had never run so fast! But then, he had never been so frightened!

In desperation Garfield leaped high and grabbed the end of a chain dangling above the floor. He swung like an orange pendulum while Pitch circled below.

"Now what?" thought Garfield. He noticed that the chain ran up to a pulley, then down to a winch nearby. And that gave him an idea.

He inched higher on the chain, then called to Pitch, "Hey, Fleabait! You're a disgrace to dogdom! You couldn't catch a fire hydrant!"

Enraged by Garfield's taunts, Pitch jumped high into the air, his jaws snapping shut on the chain just below Garfield. At that instant, Garfield threw himself at the winch and yanked the control lever. With a screech the winch spun into action. The chain went up, taking the surprised Doberman with it! In moments the dog was hanging by his teeth fifty feet above the floor!

"Dogs...they're so easy," said Garfield as he scampered away.

Garfield fetched the key from the Petman's bedside and unlocked the cages. The grateful animals spilled out. "Polly wants to thank you," said Tia. "I mean, *Tia* wants to thank you!" She stretched her wings and flew away.

Odie gave Garfield a big, sloppy kiss.

"Save the sentiment," said Garfield. "Come on! We've got to get out of here before the Doberman drops in on us!"

With Garfield and Odie in the lead, the animals rushed toward the exit.

"We're in luck!" shouted Garfield. "The Petman must be an absent-minded menace. He left the door open!"

And then the door slammed shut.

"Going somewhere, my pets?"

The Petman had returned!

"What's this?" said the Petman, staring at Garfield. "The fat cat who didn't want to play with me. Did you come to visit your friend? Well, I promise to make your stay as unpleasant as possible." The Petman picked up a piece of broken pipe and advanced toward the cowering animals.

"I'm warning you, Petman," said Garfield. "I bruise easily."

Suddenly a siren blared outside. "Come out with your hands up!" a voice called.

The Petman froze. "The cops!" he gasped. "I've got to get out of here!" The Petman burst out the door and raced past his van, heading straight for the river. He dove into the water and swam away!

Garfield and Odie peeked outside. There was no sign of the Petman. In fact, the street was deserted. "What happened to the police?" wondered Garfield.

At that moment Tia flapped down beside Garfield. "Polly watches a lot of police shows," said the parrot. "Freeze, hairball!" And she began to imitate a police siren.

"It was *you*!" cried Garfield. "You scared the Petman away. You're a hero!"

"Takes one to know one," replied the parrot, and Odie barked in agreement.

"Thanks," said Garfield. "Now follow me. Nice pets like us don't belong in a place like this."

With Garfield in the lead, the pets marched away from the docks, happy to be heading home.

The End

Story Time with
Clifford®

T3-AKX-953

SCHOLASTIC INC.

One day, Clifford went to school
with Emily Elizabeth.

He couldn't fit inside the school. But he could still watch from outside.

Clifford was so excited to listen to story time.

Later that day, Clifford told his friends how great story time was.

"I think we should start our own story time,"
Clifford suggested. Everyone agreed.

When Emily Elizabeth got home from school, Clifford exclaimed, "Story time is my favorite time!"